Go to the back of the book for your thrilling snakes and ladders board game!

Captain Flinn
and the
Pirate Dinosaurs
~☠~
Missing Treasure!

Written by
Giles Andreae

Illustrated by
Russell Ayto

MARGARET K. McELDERRY BOOKS
NEW YORK LONDON TORONTO SYDNEY

For Ned—G. A.
For my mother and
father—R. A.

A Note from the Author

By the way, there is a dinosaur in this
book called the **Giganotosaurus.**
It might be a good idea if you learn how
to say it now.

Take it bit by bit . . .

Gee – GA – no – to – SOR – us.

That's it!

Giganotosaurus!

Margaret K. McElderry Books
An imprint of Simon & Schuster Children's Publishing Division
1230 Avenue of the Americas, New York, New York 10020
Text copyright © 2007 by Giles Andreae
Illustrations copyright © 2007 by Russell Ayto
First published in Great Britain in 2007 by Puffin Books,
a publishing division of Penguin Books Ltd.
First U.S. edition, 2008
The text for this book is set in Jacoby Light.
The illustrations for this book are rendered in watercolor and ink.
Manufactured in China • 10 9 8 7 6 5 4 3 2 1
CIP data for this book is available from the Library of Congress.
ISBN-13: 978-1-4169-6745-3 ISBN-10: 1-4169-6745-1

Flinn's board— KEEP OFF!

This is Flinn. Flinn LOVES dinosaurs.

Tomorrow is a very special day because Flinn's teacher, Miss Pie, is taking his class to see the dinosaur skeletons at the museum.

"Here we are!" said Miss Pie. "Now, remember— stay together and **don't touch anything!"**

Flinn's class followed the museum guide to the Skeleton Room.

"**Wow!**" said Flinn to his friends, Pearl, Tom, and Violet. "That one looks really *scary.*"

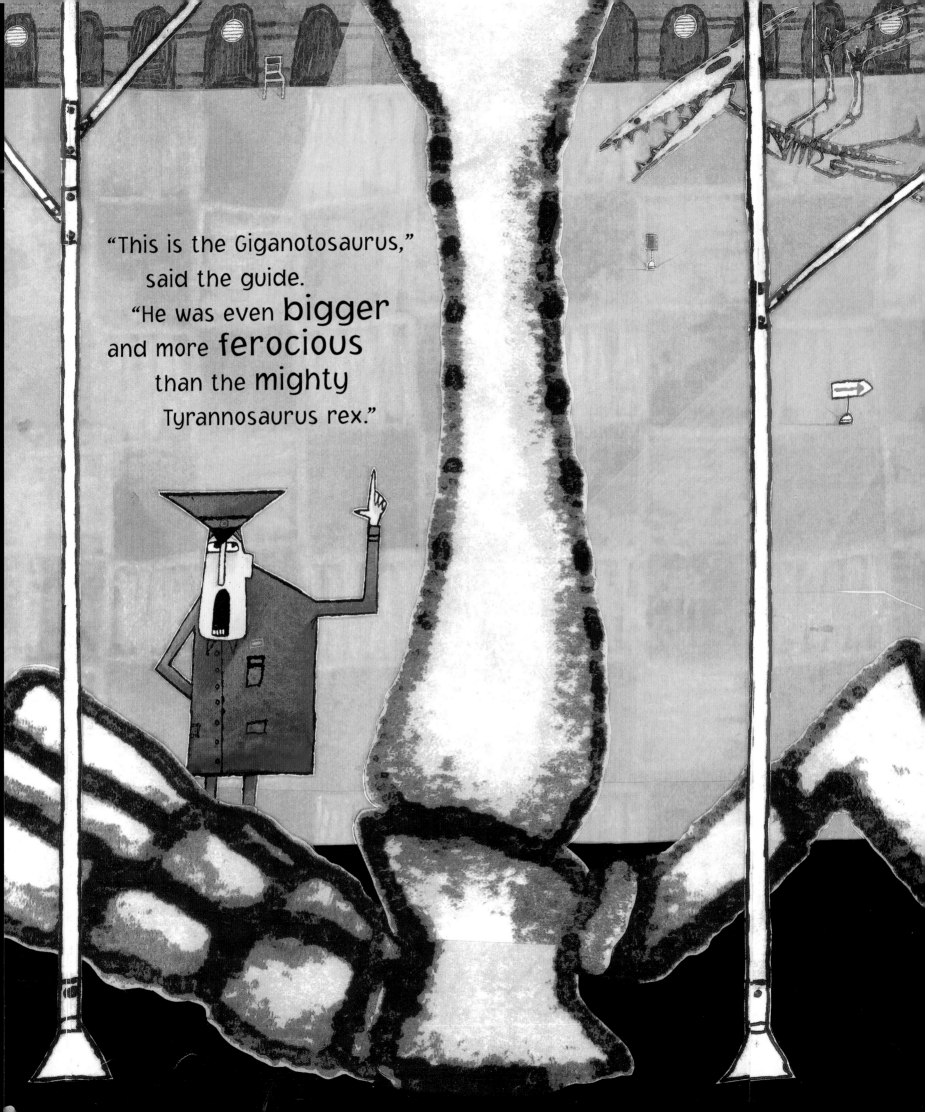

In the next room, there was a big glass case.
But it was completely EMPTY!

"It used to hold the
treasure of the famous pirate
Captain Rufus Rumblebelly,"
explained the guide,
"but it was **stolen** last night!"

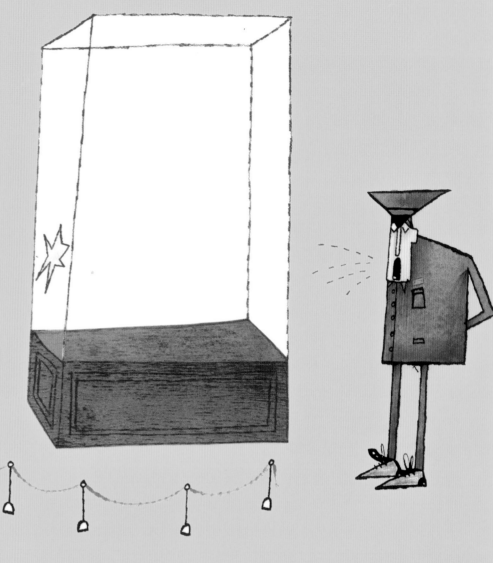

"Real pirate treasure?" said Flinn (who liked pirates
just as much as dinosaurs). "But **who** could have stolen it?"

"Look!" said Tom.
"Maybe these
peculiar feathers
are a clue. . . ."

"They seem to be leading to
that cupboard," said Pearl.

"Let's follow them!"
said Violet.

So Flinn and his friends quietly opened
the door and slipped through.

The cupboard was cold
and dark and full of
cobwebs.

"Wait a minute!"
said Flinn. "What's that?"

He bent down
and picked up a
gleaming golden coin.

"And look!
Here's another one."

"It must be the treasure!"
said Violet.

And just at that moment
the back of the cupboard fell away
and Flinn and his friends
all
tumbled

out . . .

"What treasure?" asked Flinn
as he quickly untied the pirate.

"Why, the famous treasure of
Rufus Rumblebelly!" said the pirate.
"I'm Gordon Gurgleguts, and Rufus
Rumblebelly was my granddaddy.
I took the treasure from the museum—
just to have a little look—but then
SOMEONE stole it from me!!"

"That's amazing!" said Flinn.
"We're looking for the treasure too!
We'll help you find it,
but only if you promise
to take it straight
back to the museum."

"All right," said Gurgleguts.
"I promise."

"But who stole it?"
   asked Flinn.
"I don't know," said Gurgleguts.
   "But I did hear a strange song
as they sailed away.
   "It went:

'Yo ho ho! ♪♫

♪ Yo ho ho!

Bag o' Bones Island ♪

♪♫ Here we go!'"

"Then that's where **we'll** go!"
said Flinn. "To Bag o' Bones
Island! Come on, everyone!"
   "Aye, aye!" said Gurgleguts.
   "And why don't YOU be our captain?
Here—take my hat."

So Captain Flinn took the helm and they swiftly set sail for Bag o' Bones Island.

"Island ahoy!" shouted Pirate Violet from the crow's nest.

"Follow me, everyone," said Captain Flinn. "There's thick jungle ahead and we don't want anyone to get lost. . . ."

"Gurgleguts? Gurgleguts?"

"WHERE ARE YOU?"

"Wait," said Pirate Pearl. "What's that noise?"

In front of them was a clearing. Captain Flinn peered into it and shuddered.
"Pirates!" he said. "But they're not just ordinary pirates. They're . . .

"...PIRATE DINOSAURS!"
And he was right!
There was ...

A PIRATE DIPLODOCUS ...

A PIRATE STEGOSAURUS ...

A PIRATE TRICERATOPS ...

AND A GREAT BIG PIRATE
TYRANNOSAURUS REX.

Beside the pirate dinosaurs
was a huge pile of gleaming
treasure. And next to the
treasure, tied up from head
to foot, was GURGLEGUTS.

The pirate dinosaurs were singing a terrible song.

"We've stolen all the treasure.
    We'll use it at our leisure.

And won't it be a pleasure
    For us all to live like kings!

"Stop!" yelled Captain Flinn.
"Untie my friend **immediately!**"

"We couldn't possibly do that,"
said the Tyrannosaurus rex,
squeezing a huge dollop of
tomato ketchup onto Gurgleguts's head.
"Because we're going to

EAT HIM UP!"

"Well, then, you slimy seafaring sausages,"
said Captain Flinn, drawing his sword,
"you nasty *noodle-brained* nincompoops,
you dirty *dastardly* dunderheads—
you're going to have to

eat

me

first!

ATTACK!"

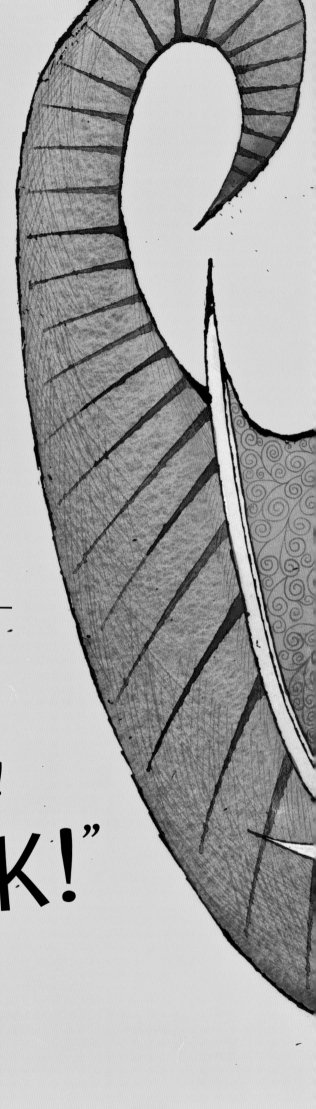

Crash!

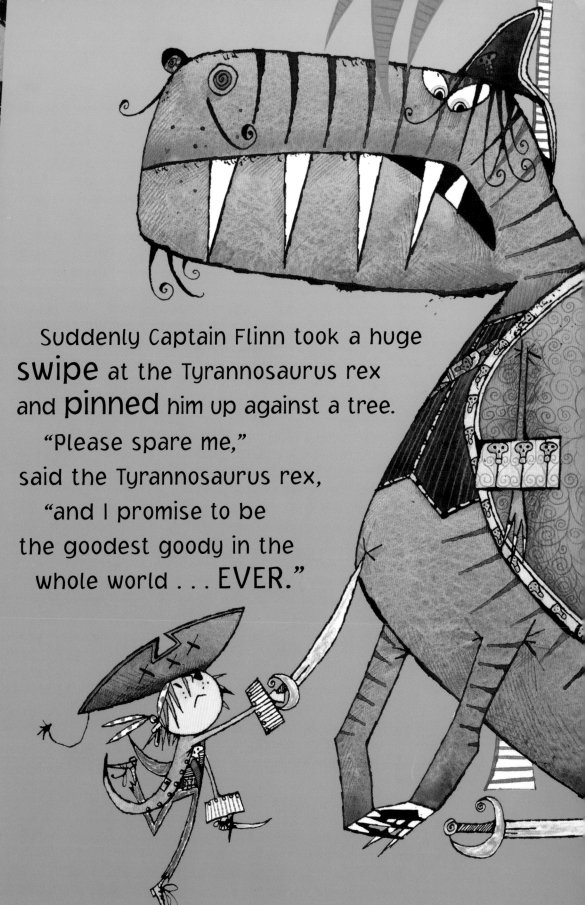

Suddenly Captain Flinn took a huge **swipe** at the Tyrannosaurus rex and **pinned** him up against a tree.
"Please spare me,"
said the Tyrannosaurus rex,
"and I promise to be
the goodest goody in the
whole world . . . EVER."

"You great **big fibber!**" said Captain Flinn.
"Fibber, eh?" said the Tyrannosaurus rex angrily.
"Well, then, I think it's time you met my cousin!"

The ground began to shake, and an **enormous shadow** fell over the island.

There was the hugest, **fiercest**, most **terrifying-looking** dinosaur in the whole world.

"Gulp," said Captain Flinn. "Who are you?"

"I'M GIGANOTOSAURUS," roared the dinosaur, "and I'm so BIG and TOUGH and SCARY that nothing in the whole world ever frightens me!"

Then suddenly . . .

"Well, shiver me timbers," said Flinn. "Fancy a big old dinosaur being scared of a teeny-weeny spider!"

HHH!"

cried the Giganotosaurus.

"Spider! Spider! Help! HEEEELP!!"

A tiny spider was hanging from Captain Flinn's pirate hat.

"They're just so creepy and crawly," wailed the Giganotosaurus. "Keep him **away** from me—**please!**"

In all the commotion Captain Flinn saw his chance.

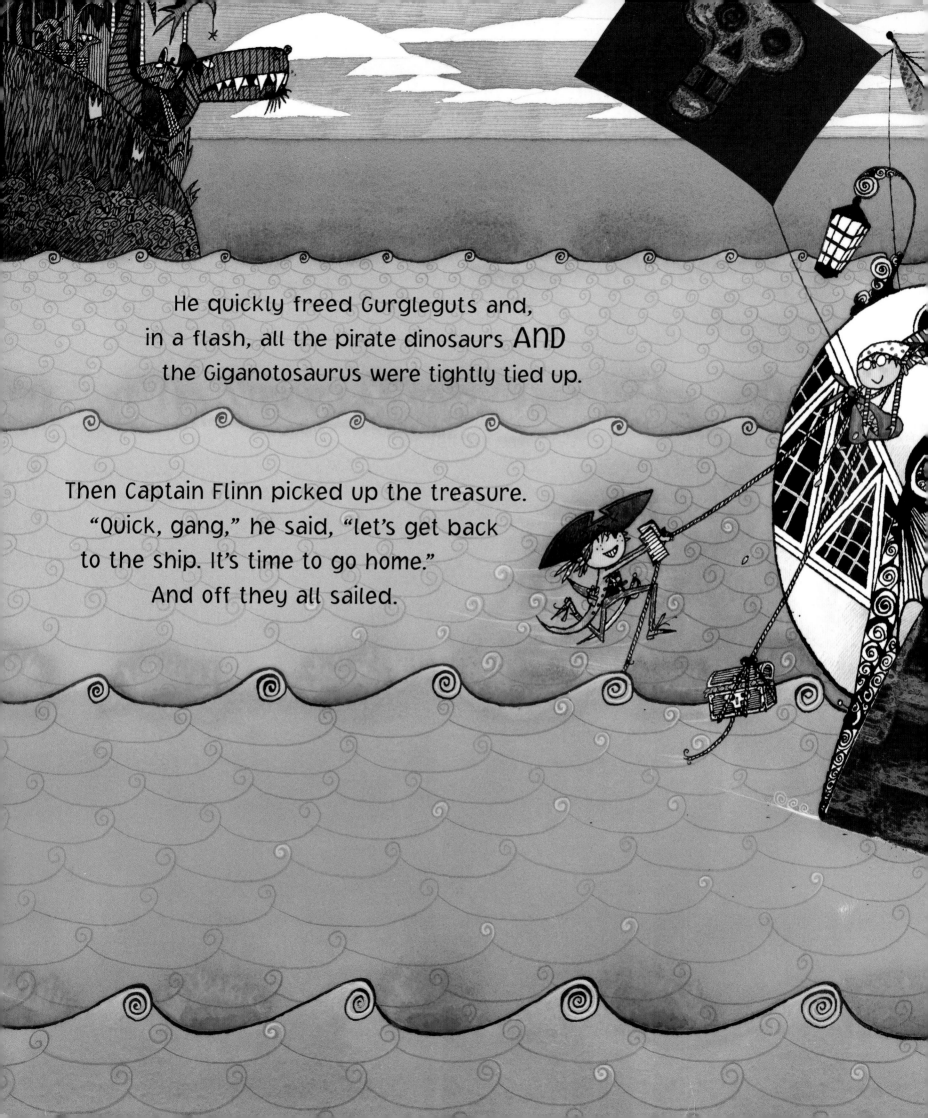

He quickly freed Gurgleguts and,
in a flash, all the pirate dinosaurs AND
the Giganotosaurus were tightly tied up.

Then Captain Flinn picked up the treasure.
"Quick, gang," he said, "let's get back
to the ship. It's time to go home."
And off they all sailed.

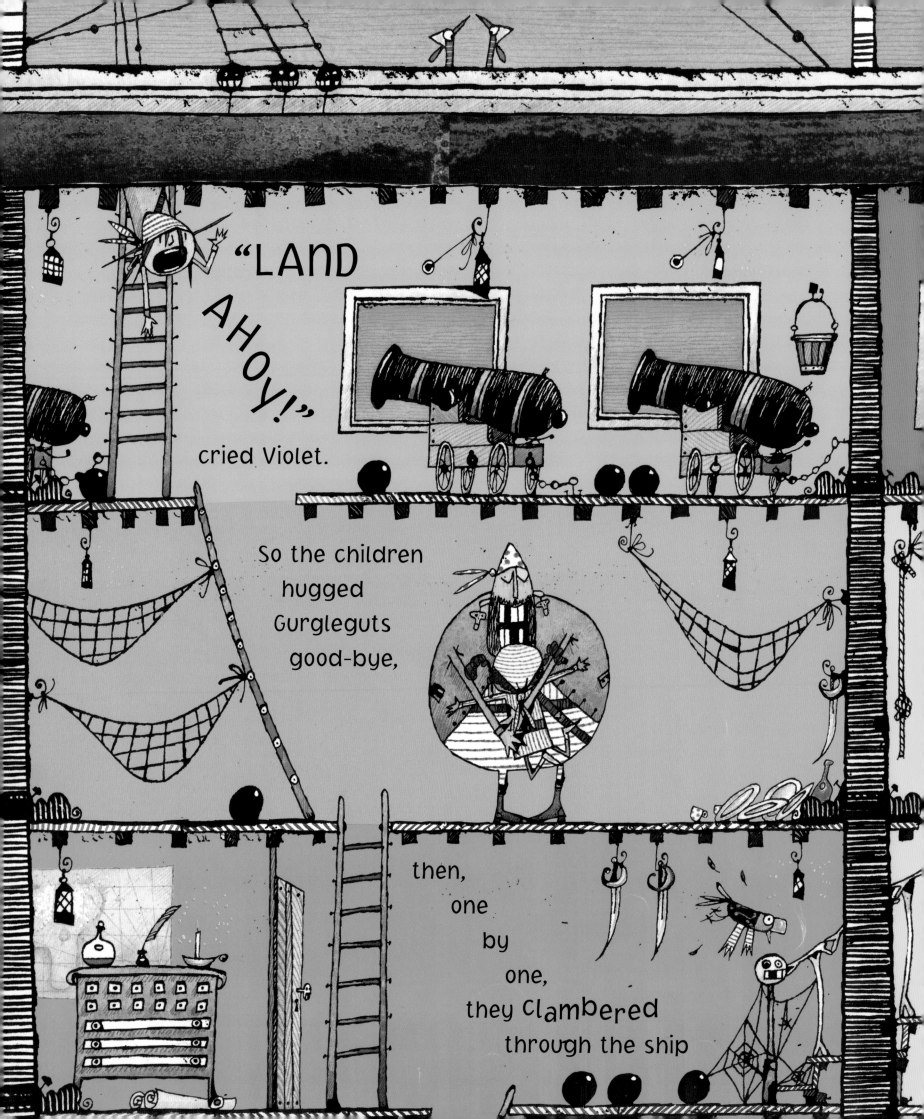

"LAND AHOY!" cried Violet.

So the children hugged Gurgleguts good-bye,

then,
one
by
one,
they clambered through the ship

into the open cupboard . . . .

. . . and back
into the museum.
"Wherever have you been?"
said Miss Pie.
"We've found the missing
treasure!" said Flinn.
"My goodness!" said the
museum guide. "Well done!
But WHO stole it?"

"It's a long story," said Flinn. "But it ended up in the hands of some pirates. Oh, and they weren't just pirates, they were PIRATE DINOSAURS!"

"Pirate dinosaurs!"
The guide laughed.
"That's the silliest thing I've heard in my whole life!
Pirate dinosaurs indeed!"

"And just for your information," added Flinn, "I can tell you something about your Giganotosaurus. He was frightened of spiders. Very frightened indeed."

Snakes and Ladders!

Heave-ho, me hearties! Are YOU brave
enough to face the dangers of the deep?

You will need

- ☠ A die
- ☠ Pieces of eight—plunder your piggy bank
  for coins to use as counters!
- ☠ 2–4 pirates

How to play

Put on your pirate hats and decide who is going to go first.

Roll the die and move your coin the number of spaces shown.

If you land on the bottom of some rigging, climb all the
way to the top. Oo-AAAR-R-GGGGH!

But if you land on a sea serpent's head, slide all
the way down to its tail. SEAFARING SAUSAGES,
IT'S TIME TO WALK THE PLANK!

The first pirate to reach the treasure is the winner!

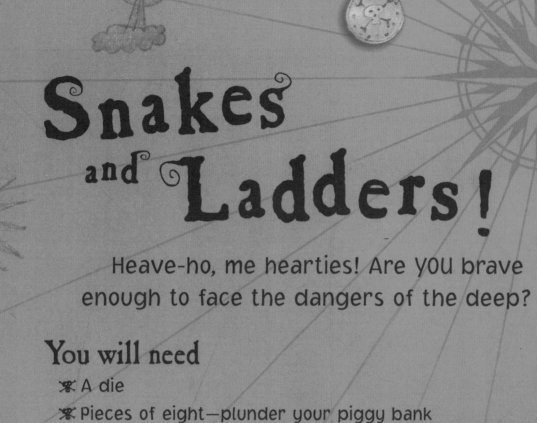